Ragged Island Mysteries

Pr~~~f
of N

by Michelle Dionetti

The Wright Group®

For Jennifer, my fairy godmother,
and for Nina, my princess,
and for Ernest, my true prince

Proof of Magic
©2000 Wright Group Publishing, Inc.
Text © Michelle Dionetti
Illustrations by Taylor Bruce

Ragged Island Mysteries
©2000 Wright Group Publishing, Inc.

The Wright Group
19201 120th Avenue NE
Bothell, WA 98011
www.WrightGroup.com

Printed in the United States of America

10 9 8 7 6 5 4 3 2 1

ISBN: 0-322-01579-0
ISBN: 0-322-01649-5 (6-pack)

Jinx

Allie

Liz

Drew

Puffin

CONTENTS

1

STONE HOUSE

Was everything ready? Liz French checked the Rocky Point Bed and Breakfast dining room. Tables set? Orange juice squeezed? Yes.

It was the Thursday before Labor Day weekend: the last weekend of summer. The bed and breakfast was full of sleeping guests. They'd want breakfast soon. There was only one thing left for Liz to do. She went upstairs to wake her sixteen-year-old sister, The Beautiful Marla.

"It's six, Marla," she said.

Marla stirred. Her honey blond hair spread across the pillow like an angel's wing.

"Get up," said Liz.

Breakfast began at seven. It took Marla at least forty minutes to dress. It took Liz five.

Marla turned over, beautifully. Liz grabbed a glass of water from the bedside table. She looked at the glass—half full. How much should she dump on her sister?

Liz tipped the glass. The first drops hit Marla's neck.

"Yi!" yelped Marla.

Liz grabbed her running shoes and headed out. Her jobs were done. Marla was awake. The table was ready, all but the food. Food was Ma's job. Serving was Marla's. Liz was free until ten.

Fog! Liz loved running in fog! She loved how you could see fog in front of you, but when you ran to it, it moved. She loved knowing no one could see Ragged Island from the mainland. In fog, the island was a secret, unless you happened to live on it.

A hinge squeaked next door. Liz's cousin Jinx and his dog Chief came out of the fog like ghosts. Liz ran up to say hi.

"Ready for the Day of Doom?" Jinx asked.

"Don't remind me," said Liz.

He meant next Tuesday, the first day of school. Liz and Jinx were not only cousins, and next-door neighbors, but classmates.

"Did you get the list for Lauren's party?" he asked.

Liz nodded. Lauren McBride was their classmate. She was giving a Start of School party Saturday. She'd invited all thirteen sixth graders. The list was for a scavenger hunt. They had to find the things on the list and bring them to the party. The prize would be for the most original collection.

"I know the list by heart," said Jinx.

"A frog, but not a real frog.

"A jewel, but not jewelry.

"A code, but not Morse code.

"A book, but not a reading book.

"Music, but not recorded music.

"Something alive that's smaller than a quarter.

"A wheel, but not a toy's wheel.

"Proof of magic.

4

"I'm almost done," Jinx bragged.

Liz didn't believe him. Sometimes Jinx said stuff just to get people going.

"Right," she said. "Proof of magic?"

"Except proof of magic," Jinx said. "Unless you count Chief. He's a dog, but he knows English."

"That's not magic. That's brains," said Liz.

Chief woofed that he agreed.

"See? Proof of brains," said Liz.

Jinx laughed. "How are you and Allie doing with your lists?"

Besides Jinx, Allie Davies was Liz's best friend.

"Allie says she has four things done," said Liz.

"Done?" said Jinx. "Is she making them?"

"Probably."

That would be like Allie. So far, Liz had a

frog-shaped pencil sharpener and a notebook. And she planned to plant a tiny flower in a pot for the live small thing.

"Drew told me he might not have time to play," said Jinx. "But he'll play."

Liz nodded. She knew Drew Ellis almost as well as Jinx did. Drew hated things that weren't clear. He would play, though, once he saw the list was a kind of joke. Drew liked a good joke.

"Hold Chief," said Liz. "I want to start."

Jinx grabbed Chief's collar. Chief liked to run with Liz.

"Where are you going?" asked Jinx.

"Stone House," Liz answered.

"Is it still empty?"

Liz nodded. Stone House had been empty since May. That's when Mrs. Hall, the owner, had to move into the nursing home in Bellport. Liz and other islanders liked to jog past Stone House. It had beautiful grounds. And a path behind it led through the woods to the east coast of Ragged Island.

"Too bad we can't have the party there!" said Jinx. "What a place for a scavenger hunt! Maybe we'd find jewels that are jewelry!"

"Yeah," said Liz. "I wonder where Mrs. Hall's jewels went?"

All of Ragged Island knew the story. Mrs. Hall had a husband, a daughter, and a fortune in jewels. The husband died. Then the daughter ran off—with the jewels, said Mrs. Hall. No, said the daughter.

Ma said the women hadn't spoken in twenty years, because they were both so stubborn.

Liz headed into the fog. She heard the foghorn in the bay and a bell buoy clang and her own footsteps. She thought she heard her heart. Her heartbeats were footsteps inside her.

There was only one thing wrong with running: it was too easy to think. And these days all Liz could think about was Ma and Pop's divorce. The divorce was new, not even six months. Liz still wasn't used to it.

Stone House was the only place on Ragged Island Liz felt safe right now. Not that home on Rocky Point was unsafe—just sad. Home had been sad since Pop left it. It hadn't been exactly happy before that. Pop and Ma had fought all the time. Liz hated that they fought. But she didn't fight with them. She had been happy.

Then they decided to divorce. Pop moved off-island to Bellport. Bellport was the town on the mainland end of the ferry route. That left Ma, Liz, and The Beautiful Marla at Rocky Point Bed and Breakfast. They were alone with five guest rooms in their farmhouse home and five one-room cabins in the orchard behind it.

Liz saw the handmade sign for Tag-Along Lane, the private road to Stone House. Then she saw a new sign—*FOR SALE*.

Oh, no! They couldn't sell Stone House! What about Mrs. Hall?

Liz flew down Tag-Along Lane. She had met Mrs. Hall only once. Mrs. Hall was stubby like a bulldog. She had mean eyes and a mouth in a straight line. Liz didn't want to think Mrs. Hall's daughter had taken the jewels. Maybe the jewels were still somewhere at Stone House. Maybe Liz could find them! Maybe she could bring Mrs. Hall and her daughter back together!

Stone House came into view through the fog. Liz wished she lived here! She loved the little gray house! She loved the garden! She loved the path through the trees behind it! The path led to Long Beach and the wild, wild sea.

Liz dropped to the garden bench. The garden was giddy with flowers, even though no one lived here. Liz thought Mrs. Hall had hired a gardener. She'd seen a young woman here, weeding and cutting flowers. The woman had black hair down to her shoulders. She always wore a big straw hat that was round like a wheel.

Liz wished this was her garden. That's what she'd wish for if she found Lauren's proof of magic. She'd wish this was her garden, her house, and her whole family lived here with her. Even Pop.

Liz heard a car. Was it coming down Tag-Along Lane? She ran into the woods. She hid behind a fat spruce and looked back.

She saw a red car, brand new, with one person inside. The car stopped. The driver got out.

It was Pop!

2

A GLINT OF GOLD

Liz ran out of the woods.

"Pop!" she shouted. "What are you doing here?"

Pop's lean face turned white. Most of the time his walk was fast and happy. Now he was still as a stick.

"Liz?" he said.

"Yeah, Pop. Me. This is one of my favorite places," said Liz.

Pop let air out of his mouth. "You scared

me, Bean," he said.

"Sorry," said Liz.

Her heart beat like a timer clock. She wasn't supposed to see him till tonight. She and Marla took the ferry to Bellport on Mondays and either Thursdays or Fridays to stay with Pop overnight.

"So come give me a hug," said Pop.

Liz did. It felt like cheating to see him by surprise. That was nuts. He was her Pop! She could hug him anytime!

"Are you selling this house?" asked Liz.

Pop was a real estate agent. He helped people buy or sell homes, land, and businesses.

"Yes," said Pop. "A Mr. Lee wants to see the house. He's on vacation here."

"There's a Mr. Lee staying at the B and B!" said Liz.

Liz had seen him when he arrived last

night. Mr. Lee was a handsome Asian man. He seemed nice, but Liz didn't want him to buy Stone House. She didn't want anyone to buy it.

"Can I see inside?" she asked.

She could tell that Pop didn't want to say yes. But since the divorce, he had a hard time saying no.

"If you're quick," he said.

"I promise!" said Liz.

He unlocked the door. Liz stepped in with a thrill. The windows! They were set deep in the walls—so deep they had stone ledges under them! Liz loved the stone ledges!

The clutter! Little tables and cupboards held wonder upon wonder. Liz loved the clutter!

And the glass! Red, blue, green—glass bottles, cups, and plates lined the dining-room window ledges. They looked like the

second item on Lauren's list for the party—
"a jewel but not jewelry." Liz loved the jewel
glass!

"Does the house buyer get all the stuff
inside too?" she asked Pop. If only she were
older! She could buy Stone House herself!

"No," said Pop. "That belongs to Mrs. Hall."

"Who gets it someday?"

"Maybe her daughter," said Pop. "If they can find her."

Maybe Liz could find her. "What's her name?" she asked.

"Penny," said Pop.

Penny Hall. Princess Penny. Liz wondered if Penny missed the velvet sofas. Or the pillows all stitched with birds. Or the stone floor in the kitchen. Liz loved the stone floor! If she had lived here when she was little, she would have pretended each stone was a kingdom!

"If you want to go upstairs, do it now," said Pop, "before Mr. Lee gets here."

Liz loved the crooked stairs. She would love to have any of the three bedrooms for her own. She wished she could look at each tiny treasure.

Pop whistled. Liz went back down. Mr. Lee was outside, in running shorts. Liz tried to look on the bright side. Maybe if Mr. Lee bought the house, he would let her run here.

"Thanks, Pop," she said. "I love Stone House! I wish you would buy it."

Pop looked mad, then sad. "Out of my price range," he said. He gave her a hug. "Say hi to Marla for me."

But not hi to Ma. He pointed Liz toward the back door. She went out and ran through the woods to Long Beach. The coast here was wild and rocky.

The fog had lifted. Liz sat on her favorite rock. She hated that Pop was the seller of Stone House. He had even wanted to sell their own home on Rocky Point. He and Ma used to fight about it. Pop was tired of Ragged Island. He wanted to live where there were more people and more things going on. Ma didn't want to leave the island or sell her home. Until Ma married Pop, the Rocky Point Bed and Breakfast was just the family farmhouse. Ma had grown up in it with Jinx's mother, Aunt Marie. Gramp had grown up in it. Gramp's grandfather had built it. And Pop wanted to sell it and move the family off-island. Ma wouldn't. So Pop left the island anyway.

Right now Pop wasn't far away. He lived just across Mackerel Bay. But Liz knew he really wanted to move someplace else. Someplace bigger than Portland, the city he'd come from. Someplace new. Every day she wondered if he'd move farther away and meet new people. Then she'd never see him again.

Liz stopped thinking. She just watched wave after wave smash into white spray.

That way it was easy to pretend that when she went home everything would be the way it used to be when she was little, once upon a time.

A wave broke and splashed Liz's legs. The tide must be coming in. Liz decided to go to Allie's and tell her about Stone House. She ran back through the woods. Pop's car was gone. Maybe he had given Mr. Lee a lift.

Liz started down Tag-Along Lane. She thought about the jewel glass inside Stone House, and Lauren's list. Marla must have a beautiful glass something for the "jewel" on Lauren's list. So Liz had four things from the list. What in the world would she use for the last item on the list, "proof of magic"?

Liz reached the end of Tag-Along Lane. Two surprises caught her eye: the back of a woman in a straw hat, walking away fast, and a glint of gold by the roadside.

3

WHOSE KEY?

The gardener! Liz stooped for the glint of gold. A key chain! Had the woman dropped it?

The chain had a clip on one end and a brass key and gold whistle on the other. There were diamonds in the whistle, one on each side. Or not diamonds—fake jewels. More jewels that were not jewelry.

Liz clipped the key chain to her shorts. Maybe she could catch up to the gardener. Liz ran her fastest, but it was no use. The woman was gone.

Now Liz had more to tell Allie! She turned onto Moody Road. Liz liked the long spaces between houses here. First came a house or two, then woods or a field. She waved to Lester Moody.

Lester's neighbor, Mrs. Morris, was outside too. But Liz didn't wave to her. She couldn't stand that woman! She wished she were invisible.

"Yoo-hoo!" called Mrs. Morris.

Oh, no! Mrs. Morris had seen her! Liz pretended not to hear.

"Yoo-hoo, dear!" Mrs. Morris sang out.

"I can't stop, Mrs. Morris!" called Liz.

"I just want to ask you something!" screeched Mrs. Morris.

Liz ran in place. "What?" she called. Ma would say she was being rude. Liz didn't care. Mrs. Morris didn't take polite hints.

"How's dear Jean?"

"Fine!" Ma WAS fine too. Ma was strong. Liz took after her.

"Oh? Not—too busy? Since your father—left?" asked Mrs. Morris.

Mrs. Morris pretended to be kind. But Liz knew what she really meant. She meant, "Is your mother falling apart?"

"No, she's fine, Mrs. Morris! I'll tell her you asked!"

Liz couldn't stand another minute. She took off like her shoes were on fire.

"Liz! Liz! What's that—"

But Liz was already around the curve in the road. Mrs. Morris tried to act like a nice person. But she was nuts. No matter what she said, she always wanted one of two things: to gossip, or for you to get her a job. Ma had hired her last summer to help at the bed and breakfast—a big mistake. Mrs. Morris gave them sloppy work and loud gossip. And she was nosy!

Liz was glad to reach Allie's. She wasn't worried about the Davies family being up. They were always up, because there were five kids. The newest one, Tomas, never slept.

All the Davies kids were adopted. Allie came from Korea. Daniel came from Washington, D.C. Liz couldn't remember about Ramon and Sasha. Tomas was from Guatemala.

Liz saw they already had company. Daniel was out front with his friend Owen McBride. Allie had three-year-old Sasha by the hand.

"Baby-sitting?" asked Liz.

"Do fish swim?" asked Allie.

"Yes," said Owen. He pushed up his thick glasses. "Fish swim, Allie."

"Do birds fly?" asked Allie.

"Yes," Owen said.

"Do I baby-sit night and day?"

"Oh," said Owen. "You were making a joke."

"I've been to Stone House," said Liz. She looked at Allie. "Inside it too."

"Inside?" Allie gasped. "How come? What's it like?"

Liz started to tell. Owen interrupted. "What's that gold thing?" he asked.

The key chain! Liz unclipped it.

"I found this," she said. "And I think I know who lost it,"

"Who?" asked Daniel.

"A woman in a hat," said Liz.

"A hat like a wheel?" asked Owen.

27

A hat like a wheel! There was a wheel, but not a toy wheel, for Lauren's party list! Now Liz had five things on the list.

Liz smiled at Owen. "Yes," she said. "Did you see her?"

"Not today," said Owen. "Mostly Sundays. I call her The Hat Woman."

Daniel took the key chain. He gave the whistle a blast. Liz clapped her hands over her ears.

"It works," said Allie.

"Cool!" said Daniel.

"Diamonds!" said Owen, bending close. "Are they real?"

"No," said Allie. "Give it back." She grabbed the key chain from Daniel and gave it to Liz. "I want to talk to Liz."

Liz filled Allie in on seeing Pop, on the inside of Stone House, on The Hat Woman, and even on Mrs. Morris.

"She's a nut," said Allie. "She sounds like Sasha, she asks so many questions."

"But Sasha's three," said Liz. "Mrs. Morris is a grown-up and weird. I hate her." Liz changed the subject. "Oh, Allie! I wish we could find Penny Hall!"

"Yeah," said Allie. "How could she stay away so long? Even if she is hurt and angry, Mrs. Hall is still her mother."

Both girls got quiet. Sasha showed Liz

her pretend fish. Liz said she liked the blue one. Sasha said she didn't have a blue fish. Her fish were all purple.

Ramon came outside and headed for his favorite dirt patch. Ramon liked to dig. Then Mrs. Davies came out. Tomas, the youngest, cried in her arms.

"Please, Allie?" she pleaded. "I have to finish that Web site by noon!"

"Okay, Mom." Allie went for Tomas.

"I have to design an Internet page for a new client," Mrs. Davies told Liz.

Allie's mom was a graphic artist. She worked at home. Boy, did she work!

"I have to go," said Liz. "I'll call you tomorrow when I get back from Pop's."

She ran home.

"Where were you?" asked Marla when she burst into the kitchen.

"Is it ten already?" asked Liz. Was she

late? It could be midnight, for all she knew. So much had happened!

"It's ten minutes to ten!" said Marla.

She wasn't late. She was early!

"I'll go change clothes," said Liz.

"You don't have time to change!" said Marla. "Mrs. Morris is in the dining room! She says she wants her key chain back!"

4

A SURPRISING FIND

The key chain! Liz unclipped it.

"Don't tell her I have it, okay Marla?" she said. "I doubt it's hers. I think it belongs to the Stone House gardener."

"Okay," said Marla. "But go get her out of the dining room! She's driving the guests crazy!"

Liz heard Mrs. Morris's voice.

"...ran better when I worked here!" Mrs. Morris said. "I think they still need me."

Like a brick banana, they needed her! Liz found Ma and some guests trapped in the dining room with Mrs. Morris. Mrs. Morris had her arms up like a scarecrow. The guests only wanted to sip coffee in peace.

Mr. Lee wasn't in the room. Gramp was there, though. Gramp was Ma's father and Jinx's mother's father. He lived around the point.

"Hi, Mrs. Morris," said Liz.

The scarecrow turned around. She stared at Liz with glassy eyes. Liz tried not to shudder.

"Come into the kitchen with me," said Liz. "So I can work while we talk."

She walked out. She hoped Mrs. Morris would follow her. After a minute she heard Mrs. Morris come down the hall. She was as quiet as a buffalo.

"Want coffee, Mrs. Morris?" asked Liz. "Tea?"

"What I want is that key chain!" said Mrs. Morris.

Was that why Mrs. Morris had called after her this morning? Because she'd seen the key chain? Liz tried stalling.

"What key chain?"

"Don't you try that on me, Liz French!" said Mrs. Morris. "The one I saw on you this morning! Just like hers!"

Liz thought, "Just like whose?" but she wasn't about to ask.

Mrs. Morris had come too close. She leaned toward Liz and stuck her fat chin out.

Liz was so scared she got angry. She had to bite her tongue to keep her temper.

Marla stood behind Mrs. Morris and made gross faces.

Now Liz had to bite her cheeks to keep from laughing.

"Where is it?" hissed Mrs. Morris.

"I took it to my friend's," said Liz.

"What friend, dear?"

Liz wasn't about to answer that! She couldn't believe the key was Mrs. Morris's. Why did the woman want it? "What's it a key to?" she asked.

"Never mind that," said Mrs. Morris.

"It's yours?" asked Liz. Maybe it really was Mrs. Morris's. "A key chain with a gold…bird…on it?"

Mrs. Morris's face didn't change. She didn't say there was a whistle on the key chain, not a bird. So the key wasn't hers! But Mrs. Morris knew something about the key chain. Or she had some crazy idea about it.

Mrs. Morris moved a step closer. Liz smelled cabbage breath. "Tell me your friend's name," said Mrs. Morris. "I'll go get the key now."

Marla took Mrs. Morris's arm. She used her sweetest tone.

"Now, Mrs. Morris. Let Liz check about the key herself," she said. "She knows you want it! She won't forget!"

Marla sounded sweet. But she had Mrs. Morris out the door in no time.

Gramp came in from the dining room. "Gone, is she?" he said.

"Thanks to Marla," said Liz.

"That woman blusters like a hurricane," said Gramp.

"I hate her," said Marla. "So snoopy!"

Ma whisked in. "Thank heaven that woman is gone!" she said. "How did we ever stand her?

"Now, I want to bake some muffins," Ma continued. "Cabin 3 needs to be cleaned. The flower beds need to be weeded. This place needs a vacuum. Who wants to do what?"

"I don't have time to clean!" said Marla. "I have to pack. We're going to Pop's, remember?"

Ma frowned, like always when someone said the word *Pop*.

"It's Labor Day weekend, Marla, and your

father isn't here to help. Starting this bed and breakfast was his idea, not mine. But I get to run it now, whether I want to or not. And unless you get your work done here, you are not going to your father's until the last ferry out. Is that clear?"

Marla muttered something rude. But she was smart enough not to say it too loud. "I'll do the cabin," she said.

"And I'll check it before you leave for your father's," said Ma.

Marla muttered again. Gramp scolded her. Liz was glad to go for the vacuum. She met Mr. Lee in the upstairs hall. He had on work clothes.

"Are you checking out, Mr. Lee?" asked Liz.

"No," said Mr. Lee. He didn't say where he was going, though.

"How did you like Stone House?" asked Liz.

Mr. Lee gave her a funny look.

"I run too," said Liz. "I saw you."

"Ah!" Mr. Lee still looked unhappy. He smiled a smile that wasn't a smile. "It's a small island, yes? I guess when you live here, everyone knows what you do."

"Pretty much," said Liz.

"A friend told me about Ragged Island," said Mr. Lee. "It's very pretty. But she didn't say how small."

He went away quickly. He was heading for a ferry, Liz guessed. Since he was out, she could vacuum his room. It was very neat. The only thing out of place was a card on the floor. Liz picked it up. It had a Bellport phone number but no name. It was an easy number to remember, too, ending in 3111. Liz put the card on the dresser. She was vacuuming another guest's room when she got a wild idea.

Mr. Lee said a friend had told him about Ragged Island. He had asked to see Stone House.

Could his friend be Penny Hall?

5

THE MISSING JEWELS

Liz tucked the key chain into her backpack to bring to Pop's.

"Mrs. Morris sure wanted that!" said Marla. "You think it's hers?"

"If it is, why didn't she know it's got a whistle on it?" said Liz. "Not a bird?"

"Yeah," said Marla from the closet. "But why doesn't she think it's yours?"

Her voice sounded like it came from inside a paper bag.

"Huh?" said Liz.

"If I saw you with a key chain that wasn't mine, I would think it was your key chain," said Marla.

Wow, Marla had a point! Liz hadn't even thought of that! "Maybe she knows whose key it really is," Liz said.

"Whose?" Marla asked. She held up two shirts. It took Marla hours to pack. It took Liz five minutes. She put a change of clothes and a book into her backpack. She had pajamas at Pop's and her own toothbrush—the usual stuff. A set at Ma's, a set at Pop's. But only one Liz.

"I don't know whose key," said Liz. "But I think it's the gardener's."

"What gardener?" Marla asked.

"A woman in a straw hat."

"Oh. Do you think Mrs. Morris knows her?" asked Marla. "Or do you think Mrs.

Morris knows what the key goes to?"

Two good ideas! A record for Marla!

"But if she knows what the key goes to, why didn't she tell me?" Liz asked.

"Because she doesn't want you to know," said Marla.

Now Liz had too much to think about. Why wouldn't Mrs. Morris want Liz to know? Unless Mrs. Morris didn't own the lock the key went to. Unless she wanted to unlock something that wasn't hers and that she didn't want Liz to know about.

"I'll show the key to Pop," said Liz. "Maybe he's seen it. Hurry up, Marla! You've got to get that cabin clean before the new guests arrive!"

"I know, I know, I'm going to," said Marla.

Liz couldn't do anything to hurry Marla, but she could weed. She went downstairs.

The kitchen was busy. Ma had her hair tied back to keep it out of the muffin batter. It was long and wiry like Liz's. Gramp fiddled with the dishwasher.

"Ma?" asked Liz. "How long has Mrs. Morris lived here?"

"On the island? Two years, I think," said Ma.

"Three," said Gramp.

"Maybe she had relatives here once," said Ma. "She does remind me of someone. But I can't think who."

"She reminds me of a circus clown," said Gramp.

"Pa!" said Ma.

"Gramp!" giggled Liz.

Someone rang the handbell out front.

"I'll bet it's that Mr. Lee again!" said Ma. "He keeps ringing the bell to ask me questions. Can we get fresh fruit here in winter? Do I know a Mrs. Spencer?"

Mrs. Spencer? Who was Mrs. Spencer? Liz went down the hall to find out. But Mr. Lee wasn't back. It was some other guest. Liz answered her question.

Next, Liz went out to the garden shed. She got clippers and the wheelbarrow. Weeding bored her. Plus she had allergies, so sometimes it made her sneeze. No wonder Mrs. Hall had a gardener.

Jinx and Chief were outside with Drew Ellis and a tape recorder. Liz always got a kick out of seeing Jinx and Drew together. Drew was big. He towered over Jinx. But Jinx moved twice as fast.

"What are you guys doing?" she called.

"Winning the scavenger hunt!" called Jinx. "What are you doing?"

"Working," said Liz. She wished she had time to win scavenger hunts.

"We'll help," said Drew.

"We will?" said Jinx.

"Sure," said Drew.

Jinx made a face, but he put Chief inside and followed Drew over. Chief liked to dig. He was not allowed anywhere near the bed and breakfast flowerbeds.

"We have to cut the dead flowers off too," said Liz.

"All right," said Jinx. He grabbed the clippers. "Tell us a story while we work."

Liz told them about Stone House being sold. She told about seeing The Hat Woman and finding the key. And about Mrs. Morris.

"Is the key to Stone House?" asked Jinx.

Liz stopped weeding. Why hadn't she thought of that? "I don't know!" she said. "I didn't try it!"

Was that why Mrs. Morris wanted it? Because it went to Stone House? But what would Mrs. Morris want with Stone House? Liz pulled a weed. She sneezed.

"I don't care about the key," she said. She pulled another weed and sneezed. "I just want to find Penny Hall. Before Mrs. Hall sells Stone House."

"Why?" asked Drew.

"Because!" said Liz.

Because not seeing your mother or your daughter again was the saddest thing! Because losing a home hurt! She herself would sneeze her way through every weed on Rocky Point, as long as she could stay here. She wished she had worked this hard when Pop lived at home. He said he was sick of Ragged Island, but maybe he was just sick of the work. To keep Pop home Liz would have pulled every weed and clipped every dead flower. Every day. Even if it killed her.

"Know what I'd do to find Penny Hall?" said Jinx. "Pretend it's another scavenger hunt. Think of ten questions about Penny Hall. Then find the answers."

"Wow! Great idea!" said Drew.

Liz stared at Jinx. "You mean like, where did Penny Hall go?" she asked.

"No," said Jinx. "More like, what did Penny Hall like to do on Saturdays? Because when you know that, you can think of places to look for her."

"Like if she liked to sail, then maybe she has a boat now?" asked Drew.

"Right," said Jinx.

Liz started to get excited. "I can ask Mrs. Lord about Penny Hall's favorite subjects in school!" she said.

Mrs. Lord was the oldest teacher at Ragged Island School, and the one who had taught there the longest.

"What about her favorite color?" said Drew.

"What does that have to do with anything?" asked Jinx.

"Maybe she owns a car that color now!" said Drew. "And ask Mrs. Lord if she had any pen pals."

"You mean Penny pals," said Jinx.

Liz groaned.

"How about summer camps?" said Drew. "Maybe she made friends there. How about other relatives?"

"And you'd better get the story on those missing jewels, Liz," said Jinx. "The jewels might be the answer to the whole riddle!"

"Gramp!" said Liz. "He's inside!"

Gramp knew everything about everyone on Ragged island. Jinx picked up the handles of the wheelbarrow.

"The flower beds look great," he said. "I

51

say we're done! Let's go in and get the story from Gramp!"

The kitchen smelled good. Muffins cooled on racks.

"Wow, what smells so good, Aunt Jean?" asked Jinx.

Ma gave him an as-if-you-didn't-know look. "Pour yourself some milk if you want," she said, "to go with your muffins. Hi, Drew."

Drew nodded to Ma and Gramp.

"Gramp!" said Jinx. "Do you know about Mrs. Hall and her jewels?"

"Yup."

"Will you tell us?" Jinx asked.

"Well now," Gramp scratched his beard. "Louise—that's Mrs. Hall's first name—had a grandfather who used to be a jeweler down to New York City. When he died he left a bag of jewels to his little granddaughter

Louise. Little Louise kept them in a black velvet bag. You should have seen that bag opened up. The jewels looked like fire against the black."

"No kidding?" said Jinx. "A little girl with a bag of jewels?"

"What did they look like?" asked Drew. "Jewels, or pieces of glass?"

"Jewels," said Gramp. "And they sparkled something awful. Worse than a midnight of stars."

"Wo!" said Jinx.

Liz wished she could see them! "Where did she keep the bag?" she asked.

"Couldn't say," said Gramp. "Somewhere close to hand. Didn't take her but a minute to get that bag when she wanted to show her jewels. I always wondered if she hid them in the fancy carvings in the woodwork. Stone House is all carved up. Roses in the ceilings. Pineapples on the stair rails. Flowers around the fireplace."

"What finally happened to the jewels?" asked Drew.

"That's the mystery," said Gramp. "Louise grew up and married Thornton Hall. They moved into his place, Stone House. They had Penny. Louise hauled out the jewels now and then to show people.

"Thorn died when Penny was seventeen. Penny had a bucket of ideas about how to save the world. She and her Ma started to fight like jays. Penny wanted to adopt stray animals. She wanted to open a free clinic for kids. She wanted to fund a homeless shelter. Mrs. Hall said no, no, no."

"Then what?" said Liz.

"Then one day after a big fight, Penny disappeared. It took a few days for Mrs. Hall to figure out she was gone for good. That's when she looked for her bag of jewels. What she had was a bag of fakes. And that's when the whole island found out the jewels were missing!"

"Maybe something bad happened to Penny," said Liz. "Because of the jewels." She didn't want to think how bad.

"Maybe," said Gramp. "There were

55

newspaper headlines all across the state. It was a Maine state hobby—everyone was looking for Penny Hall."

"For the jewels, you mean," said Jinx.

Gramp nodded. "Maybe," he said. "Finally Penny—or someone pretending to be Penny—called Bellport News and made a statement. She said she had left home for good, but she had not taken the jewels."

"I remember that," said Ma. "Penny baby-sat for me and Marie a few times. Both of us believed her."

"What do you think, Gramp?" asked Liz. "Do you think she took them?"

"I only know they're gone without a trace," said Gramp. "So's she."

Liz's heart sank. It didn't sound good. Maybe Penny was dead. Or living in another country. Or maybe she was alive, and guilty after all!

6

THE HAT WOMAN

Uncle Rich—Jinx's dad—offered to drive Liz and Marla to the ferry landing. They had to catch the midday ferry to Bellport or wait till six for the next one. Liz was ready. But The Beautiful Marla demanded time for Hair Fashion.

Liz put her backpack in the truck bed. Next she loaded Marla's stuff. Ragged Islanders went to high school in Bellport. So after school started, Marla would stay at

Pop's an extra day during the week. She could go to school games and have more homework time. Everyone agreed The Beautiful Marla needed more homework time. Liz loaded Marla's suitcase, make-up case, and backpack.

"Planning an overseas mission?" asked Uncle Rich.

"In a way," said Liz.

Bellport was sort of overseas. She climbed into the cab of the truck. So did Chief. Jinx climbed in too.

"I'll go over on the ferry with you," he said, "to help carry stuff."

"Cool," said Liz.

Marla finally joined them. She carried her cheerleading outfit. Once they got on the ferry, Marla's stuff filled one long bench inside it.

"Pop just has to buy me a hair dryer for Bellport!" said Marla loudly. "I can't carry mine back and forth twice a week!"

Liz was sure the ferry passengers didn't care. She didn't care. She went up top with Jinx, into the salty air. They leaned on the rail and watched Ragged Island shrink. Seagulls followed the ferry's wake.

"Seagulls are stupid," said Liz.

"They think every boat is a fishing boat," Jinx agreed. "What are you going to do when you get to Bellport?"

"Go to Shady Rest nursing home to see

if I can visit Mrs. Hall."

"No kidding!" said Jinx.

"I want to ask if she's heard from her daughter," said Liz.

"She's going to bite your head off," warned Jinx.

"Maybe. But I have to try," said Liz.

"How about we all get together tomorrow afternoon and make a plan to find the jewels?" asked Jinx.

"You mean to find Penny Hall!" said Liz.

"Her too," said Jinx. "I'll call Drew and Allie."

"Okay," said Liz. "Maybe I'll learn something from Mrs. Hall that will tell us what to look for."

Pop was at the ferry landing. The Beautiful Marla left the bags to Liz and Jinx. She carried her cheerleading outfit.

"Pop," she said, "I need a hair dryer."

"Why? Your hair isn't wet," said Pop.

"Pop!" cried Marla.

Pop took Marla's suitcase and Marla's backpack. That left Jinx Marla's pink make-up case. Liz laughed at Jinx's frown.

Bellport covered a steep hill. Marla talked about a new hair dryer all the way up it. She talked across Dock Street, then Main Street, then Court Street. Pop lived at 151 High Street, between Court Street and Ridge Street at the top of town.

"Cool," said Jinx, when they reached Pop's apartment.

"I guess," said Liz.

She would love Pop's place if she didn't hate that he lived in it. And if she thought he would live here always, or at least until she was grown. But she knew he wouldn't. Already he talked about wanting to have more room, even though he had the whole top floor of a three-story house.

Jinx looked out each window. "Ragged Island looks like a goosebump on the ocean!" he said.

Liz wished she were back on the goosebump.

"Did Mr. Lee like Stone House, Pop?" she asked.

"Hard to say," said Pop. "But he wants to see it again this weekend. And Mrs. Morris called me. She wants me to hire her to clean it."

"Don't do it!" chorused Liz and Marla.

"Don't worry!" said Pop. "I remember her 'help' all too well!"

Liz unzipped her backpack. She showed Pop the key chain. Neither Pop nor Jinx had ever seen it.

"So can we go buy me a hair dryer, Pop?" asked Marla.

"We'll see. I still have to show some houses today," said Pop.

"You mean now?" asked Liz. But they were here to visit him!

"Yup," said Pop.

He acted like it was nothing!

"I'll be back around seven," Pop said.

"We'll be fine, Pop," said Marla. "I'm going to do Liz's hair."

Over Liz's dead body!

"That's nice," said Pop.

No it wasn't! Liz watched Pop head out the door. Like always. These days, every time Liz watched Pop leave, she wondered if she'd ever see him again.

"No hair," she said to Marla. "I'm going to Shady Rest to see Mrs. Hall."

"Mrs. Hall?" said Marla. "The one from Stone House who hates her own daughter?"

"Yeah, that one," said Liz.

"But why?" asked Marla.

"Because maybe if I can find Penny Hall, she can come take care of Mrs. Hall! They'll be together! And they won't have to sell Stone House," Liz explained.

"I get the part about the house," said Marla. "I don't get the part about helping Mrs. Hall. She's sort of mean, Liz."

"It isn't for Mrs. Hall," said Liz. "It's for her daughter. What if Penny comes home after all these years? And the house she grew up in is sold?"

For once The Beautiful Marla was silent. Liz knew Marla had heard all those fights last year too, the ones about selling the Rocky Point Bed and Breakfast.

"I wish I could go with you," said Jinx, "but I have to catch the next ferry back."

"I'll go," said Marla. "I need the exercise. Later I'll do your hair."

Liz could fight the hair fight later. She went downstairs with Jinx. She'd wait outside. Marla couldn't just leave. She had to do a face tune-up first.

Some guy went down High Street playing a flute.

"Hey!" said Jinx. "Music, but not recorded music! What are you doing for music, Liz? I have a harmonica."

Liz shrugged.

"You could sing," said Jinx.

"Oh, right, so you could laugh!" Liz could barely carry a tune.

"Oh, I forgot!" said Jinx. "It has to be music!"

Liz tried to punch him. She missed. Jinx started down the long hill.

"See you tomorrow!" he called.

Liz watched Jinx get smaller until he turned toward the ferry landing and loped out of sight. She wished she could go with him, back to Ragged Island. Bellport was a great town, if you liked towns. The town limits were just over the hill. Then the town turned to country fast. Bellport had shops for Marla and places to run for Liz. Liz used to like it a lot more before Pop moved here.

Lauren's party was coming up on Saturday. What would Liz do for music? If she still had the whistle key chain, she'd bring that. Or she'd use her lips. If a bird could whistle, so could Liz. She tried whistling "The Star Spangled Banner."

"You sound stupid," said Marla.

"Thanks, sis," said Liz. She wished she could say Marla looked stupid. But Marla looked good. Marla always looked good, even when she thought so herself.

Marla started down the hill.

"Nursing home," reminded Liz. Shady

Rest was just over the top of Ridge Road, on the way out of town.

"First can we go by this shop?" asked Marla. "And get some shampoo?"

"No," said Liz.

Marla had a shampoo collection. Shampoo bottles lined the rim of the tub at home. More lived under the sink—the rejected ones.

"It's on the way!" said Marla.

Liz gave up. Going down when you were supposed to go up was not "on the way." Marla turned left and stopped in front of a shop. Liz looked in the window. She saw candles, lotions, soaps, and wreaths of dried flowers. She could smell rose and lilac. Liz sneezed. She was allergic to roses. The shop was called Beautiful You. No wonder Marla liked it.

"Closed!" wailed Marla.

"It's after five," said Liz.

"Sage shampoo!" sighed Marla.

But Liz had her eye on the woman behind the counter. The woman was young, with black hair!

The only thing missing was the hat shaped like a wheel!

7

HINTS AND CLUES

The Stone House gardener! Liz knocked on the window. Instead of looking up, the woman turned away.

"She's closed," said Marla.

"That's her!" said Liz. "The Hat Woman!"

She held up the key. No use. The woman went through a back door.

"Don't be dumb," said Marla.

She pulled Liz's hand down. Liz sneezed again. She would come to check the woman out on Monday. She hoped the rose smell wouldn't kill her.

"Now, the nursing home," she said.

"Okay, okay." Marla started a brisk walk. "I wonder if I'll get to school faster this year?" she said.

"Because you'll walk faster?" asked Liz.

"Because I'm taller," said Marla.

They walked uphill. Marla talked about taking French. Liz thought about French. French was a kind of code. Or no; a code was a kind of language, one that someone made up and only some people knew. Liz needed a code for Saturday, for Lauren's party list.

"Marla," said Liz, "do you know any codes?"

"Morse code."

"Besides Morse code."

"The Code of Hammurabi,"

"What's that?" asked Liz.

"It's Egyptian," said Marla. "I think."

"Never mind," said Liz. She'd ask someone else. Like Chief. He'd say, "Arf! Arf! Arf!"

Liz stopped short. Chief barked in code! "Arf" for "no." "Arf Arf" for "I mean it!" And "Arf Arf Arf" for "Let me out!" She had a code!

By the time they reached Shady Rest, The Beautiful Marla was short of breath.

"I'm staying outside," she said. "Don't take forever." She sank to a bench.

Liz went in. Shady Rest was a new, low building. She asked to see Mrs. Hall. The woman at the front desk looked surprised.

"Room 202," she told Liz. "To your left."

Liz went down the hall. The floor shone. She reached room 202. A nurse came out of it. She had glasses, round cheeks, and curly hair.

71

"Is this Mrs. Hall's room?" asked Liz.

"Why yes," said the nurse. "Are you here to see her?" She looked even more surprised than the woman at the desk.

Liz nodded.

The nurse bent close. She had kind eyes. "She's a little difficult," she warned in a low voice.

"So I hear," said Liz. She took a deep breath and walked into the room.

Mrs. Hall looked smaller than Liz remembered. Her eyes were angry, and her mouth was tight.

"Who are you and what do you want?" said Mrs. Hall.

"Liz French from Ragged Island," said Liz. "My father is your real estate agent. I want to help you find your daughter." She didn't say the rest out loud. But she thought, "So you won't die before she sees you again."

"I have no daughter," said Mrs. Hall.

"Because she ran away?" said Liz.

Mrs. Hall turned red. "What do you know about it, Miss Smarty?" she asked.

"Just what Gramp told me," said Liz. "That you said Penny took some jewels. That Penny said she didn't."

Liz watched Mrs. Hall turn purple. Maybe she should call that nurse.

"Who is Gramp?" asked Mrs. Hall. She made Gramp sound like Cramp.

"Roland LaPlante."

"Him," said Mrs. Hall. "I remember him. I remember his late wife, Pauline, too. And his girls."

His girls would be Ma and Aunt Marie. Liz watched Mrs. Hall's chin quiver. She guessed Mrs. Hall didn't want to talk about her daughter. If she did, she'd be admitting she had one.

Liz's eyes filled with tears. Poor Mrs. Hall! Probably she loved her daughter somewhere in that closed-up heart!

"I'll help you find her," said Liz.

"Why?" said Mrs. Hall.

"Because she's all you have," said Liz.

She surprised herself. She thought what

she cared about was Stone House. But it wasn't the house. It was the home. Maybe Liz's parents weren't living together, but she knew she had a home with them both. In a way, she was lucky.

Now Mrs. Hall looked very old and very tired. "I got a card a year ago," she said, "from Portland."

Liz felt a rush of hope. Portland was right here in Maine! She took the key chain out of her pocket.

"Have you seen this before?" she asked.

Mrs. Hall tried to sit up. "Where did you get that?" she demanded.

"Near your house," said Liz. "Is it yours?"

Mrs. Hall pressed her lips together. "I think it's a key to my house!" she said. "Find out! Find out anything you can about my house! I want to know if things are missing. Then come back here and tell me!"

"Okay," said Liz. She wished Mrs. Hall wasn't so upset.

"And if you find…anyone…tell her to return my jewels!" said Mrs. Hall. "Then I'll forgive!"

Liz knew that "anyone" meant Penny. "What if she didn't take them?" she asked.

Mrs. Hall got red again. "No more questions!" she shouted. "And don't come back until you've found my jewels!"

Liz saw what Ma meant when she said the Halls were stubborn! What if Liz found Penny, and Penny said, "Tell my mother that first she has to apologize! Then I'll see her!"

"A daughter is worth more than jewels," said Liz.

"Out!" said Mrs. Hall.

The kind nurse came in. She shook her head at Liz. Liz got the message. It was time to go. She followed the nurse out.

"Sorry," she said. "Is it okay that she got mad? I mean, did it hurt her health?"

The nurse made a face. "It better be okay," she said, "since I've never seen her anything but mad or sad."

"Has her daughter ever come here?" asked Liz.

The nurse got an odd look.

"Ah…I've never met her," she said.

What did that mean? Never met her? Had Penny Hall tried to see her mother? Before Liz could ask more, the nurse went back into Mrs. Hall's room.

Liz went back through the lobby. The phone on the front desk rang.

"Good evening! Shady Rest!" said the woman at the desk. "No, you have a wrong number."

Liz reached the door.

"The number here is 555-3111," said the woman.

Liz stopped short. 3111! Wasn't that the number on Mr. Lee's card?

What was Mr. Lee doing with the Shady Rest phone number?

8

LOOKING FOR PENNY HALL

On Friday morning, Liz took the seven o'clock ferry to Ragged Island—the same one she'd have to take next week to school. She wished she could stay till ten. Then she could go back to Beautiful You and talk to The Hat Woman. But Rocky Point was full of guests. Ma would need help.

The Beautiful Marla refused to get up.

"I'll be working all weekend long, Liz!" she said.

So would Ma. And Liz. But Pop wouldn't make Marla get up.

"I'll get her on the eleven o'clock," he said. "After I buy her a hair dryer. Come on, Bean. I'll walk you down."

Liz told Pop about visiting Mrs. Hall. She told how Mrs. Hall wanted her to see if the key she had found fit Stone House.

"Is it okay if I try the key today?" asked Liz. "And bring Allie, Jinx, and Drew?"

"Okay," said Pop. "But if you can get inside, tell me. And leave things as you find them."

"We will," promised Liz.

It was foggy again. Liz couldn't see Ragged Island. Maybe she would sit inside the ferry this time. Fog could be cold and wet. And she still had to run home. Maybe she'd meet Mr. Lee out running.

"Pop, does Mr. Lee live in Bellport?"

asked Liz.

"Portland, I think," answered Pop.

"What does he do?" asked Liz.

"He's a jeweler," said Pop.

"A jeweler!" Liz's heart raced like a wind-up toy. "Pop! Maybe he knows where Mrs. Hall's jewels are!"

"Now there's a real stretch, Bean," said Pop.

"Or he wants to find them!" said Liz.

"Or he just wants to buy a vacation home," said Pop.

"Yeah, right," Liz thought. Mr. Lee didn't seem to like Ragged Island. It was too small and nosy for him.

"Did he ask to see Stone House in particular?" she asked.

"Yes he did," said Pop.

"Any other houses?" Liz asked.

They had reached the ferry landing. Pop

bought Liz a month's pass.

"No more about my clients," he said. "And don't decide Mr. Lee is some kind of crook. You don't know him."

Too bad. "Okay, Pop," said Liz.

"See you Monday," said Pop. "The day before the first day of school!"

"Yuck," said Liz.

She got on the ferry with lots of other people, and lots of suitcases. Most of the people were off-islanders coming for the weekend.

"Hello, Liz French!"

"Mrs. Lord!" Liz slid into the long seat next to her old teacher. "Did you spend last night on the mainland?"

"Yes, dear," answered Mrs. Lord. "With my sister. She lives just south of Bellport, you know. And our father is at Shady Rest."

Mrs. Lord was almost too old to teach. Her father must be a hundred.

"How is he?" Liz asked politely.

"Very poorly. He didn't know us."

What if Pop got too old to know who she was? Liz shivered.

"I went to Shady Rest too," she said. "To see Mrs. Hall."

Mrs. Lord looked surprised. "Louise Hall from Stone House?" she asked.

"Yes," said Liz. "I want to find Penny for her."

"Why is that, dear?"

Mrs. Lord's kind voice made Liz cry. She hoped she could answer without her own voice shaking.

"Sometimes I worry that one day Pop will move, and I'll never see him again," she said.

Mrs. Lord didn't say anything stupid like, "I don't get it." Or "Don't be silly." She just nodded. "I see how finding Penny might help that feeling," she said.

"Do you remember Penny?" asked Liz. "What was she like?"

"I taught her in second grade," said Mrs. Lord. "She didn't talk much, but you wouldn't call her quiet. She had opinions.

She brought a bird with a broken wing to school once. She brought a chipmunk in too. She said it had a hurt leg. The chipmunk wasn't hurt much. I told her to take it back where she found it. Instead she brought it home with her. 'I know it needs help, Mrs. Lord,' she told me. 'I think it will be better off without your help, Penny,' I said. 'Wild things need to survive on their own.' She was so angry with me, she didn't speak to me for a week!"

"Do you remember anything else?" asked Liz.

"She had a pretend friend, Handy."

"In the second grade?"

Mrs. Lord nodded. "She didn't care who knew it, either!"

"When was the last time you saw her?" asked Liz.

"The year she left the island," Mrs. Lord

said. She looked sad.

"Because of the jewels," said Liz.

"I never believed she took them," said Mrs. Lord. "Her treasures were empty bird's eggs or seashells, not jewels."

"Did she have any pen pals you know about?" asked Liz. "Or other relatives?"

"I never heard of any," said Mrs. Lord. "She wrote a story about a visit to a friend in Portland, though."

Liz wondered if that friend could have been Mr. Lee. "No—it couldn't be," she thought. "Mrs. Lord meant Penny Hall as a child. Not Penny Hall now."

Liz's head hurt. But at least she had an idea of what Penny Hall was like. Someone kind. Someone caring. Maybe someone who was so sure she was right, she might steal her mother's jewels. For a good cause.

The ferry docked. It wasn't foggy

anymore. Just cloudy. Liz hoped the sun would shine. Clouds made bed and breakfast guests grumpy.

She picked up Mrs. Lord's suitcase. Then she found out that Mrs. Lord liked to get off the ferry after everyone else. "I don't like to rush, dear," she said.

So Liz didn't see The Hat Woman until it was too late. And she couldn't just dump Mrs. Lord's suitcase and run! She had to get Mrs. Lord into the island taxi. By then the big straw hat was gone.

Oh, no! Probably The Hat Woman was headed for Stone House. Could she run to Stone House too? Maybe Mr. Lee was also out running. Maybe he and The Hat Woman would meet. Liz's heart skipped a beat. Maybe they knew each other! Maybe they planned to meet at Stone House!

That did it! Liz ran her best speed. She

was rewarded too, because when she got to Stone House she saw Mr. Lee. He stood in the garden and stared down the path to Long Beach.

"Hi, Mr. Lee!" Liz called. She hoped she didn't scare him to death. "That path goes out to the east end of the island!"

Mr. Lee turned. She noticed he could frown and look polite at the same time.

"Does everyone on the island come here?" he asked.

Liz shook her head. "Not really," she said. "I do, and my friend Allie, and a woman wearing a big straw hat. Do you know her?"

Mr. Lee looked back at the woods.

"No," he said. "But I just saw her. She went into the woods when I came."

"I think she just comes to tend the garden or pick the flowers," said Liz. "She has a shop in Bellport that sells dried flowers."

Mr. Lee looked thoughtful. Liz made up her mind.

"You knew about Stone House, didn't you?" she asked. "Before you came here, I mean. You know about Mrs. Hall's jewels."

Mr. Lee crossed his arms. His face didn't change. But Liz knew he was really angry.

"I don't care about the jewels," she said. "Unless they lead to Penny Hall."

"And why do you want to find Penny Hall?" asked Mr. Lee.

"Because her mother is old," said Liz. "They have to get back together before it's too late. They just have to!"

Tears filled her eyes. Now Mr. Lee looked at Liz, and Liz looked at the woods.

"Do you know Penny?" asked Mr. Lee.

"No," said Liz. Her voice shook. She hated that! She felt stupid!

Mr. Lee uncrossed his arms. "Come and sit down," he said. "Maybe you and I can help each other."

They sat on the garden bench. Mr. Lee offered his hankie.

Liz blew her nose. Now what? Did she give it back all snotty?

"Thanks," she said. "I'll wash it."

Mr. Lee almost smiled.

"Now I will tell you a story," he said. "Years ago a woman came to my shop. She was tall, with silver hair. She brought me a single diamond. She said it came from her mother's ring. She wanted to sell it and use the money to help a young friend. I paid her well. It was a beautiful stone.

"The next week the news came about Mrs. Hall's missing jewels. I thought about the diamond. But it did not match the police list of any of Mrs. Hall's jewels.

"This spring another woman came to see me. This woman wore a blond wig. She too wanted to sell me a single jewel: a ruby. I asked where she got it. She said a friend gave it to her years ago. She did not meet my eyes, so I did not believe her."

Liz took a breath. "Was she Penny Hall?" she asked.

Mr. Lee shook his head. "The woman in the wig told me her name was Miss Smith," he said. "A false name, of course. I told her I wanted to keep her ruby overnight to think about buying it. I really wanted to look through police lists of missing jewels to see if this ruby was stolen."

"Did she let you keep it?" asked Liz.

"No. She grabbed it out of my hand and left the store. Because she said she'd gotten the ruby years ago, I thought of Mrs. Hall. Had Mrs. Hall ever recovered her missing jewels? I got in touch with her."

He knew Mrs. Hall! So that's why he had the Shady Rest phone number!

"What did she tell you?" asked Liz.

"That they were still missing. I went to see her, and she gave me a detailed list. Emeralds. Sapphires. Diamonds. And rubies."

"And the women?" asked Liz. "Did Mrs. Hall know who they were?"

"I told her the first woman was tall, with a deep voice and short, silver hair. Mrs. Hall said it sounded like her old friend Ruth Handy. Mrs. Hall got an odd look. She said, 'Ruth must have really wanted the money.'"

Mr. Lee went on. "We talked about the woman in the blond wig. Mrs. Hall wondered if she was a Mrs. Spencer. Mrs. Spencer used to work at Stone House years ago. Until Mrs. Hall got tired of her prying and fired her."

"Was Mrs. Spencer working here when Penny left home?" asked Liz.

"No," said Mr. Lee. "Mrs. Hall fired Mrs. Spencer in April. Penny left in June."

Too bad! Sounded like Mrs. Spencer couldn't have taken the jewels!

"Did Mrs. Hall tell you about Stone

House?" asked Liz.

"She told me," said Mr. Lee.

"But you don't want to live here," said Liz. "You want to find the jewels!"

This time Mr. Lee did smile. "Yes," he admitted. "I am like a child! I want to find treasure!"

Liz did too. But not the jewels. She wanted to find lost love between a mother and a daughter.

"I have to go help Ma," she said.

Mr. Lee nodded. "You run a fine bed and breakfast," he said. "I will try to find that woman in the hat. I'll see what she knows about Stone House."

"My friends and I are going to come back here later," said Liz.

"To look for treasure buried in the garden?" said Mr. Lee with a smile.

"Maybe if we find the jewels," said Liz,

"Mrs. Hall will forgive Penny."

Liz thought about Mr. Lee's story on the way home. Who was the woman in the blond wig? Penny Hall? Mrs. Spencer?

"Pssst!"

Liz jumped a foot. Mrs. Morris stepped out from behind a bush.

9

CLUE PLUS CLUE EQUALS PROGRESS

"You scared me!" gasped Liz.

Mrs. Morris always scared her. It was the crazy look in those little eyes.

"I want my key!" Mrs. Morris spoke through her teeth.

The key was right in Liz's backpack. Liz thought fast.

"I don't think the key I have is yours," she said.

Mrs. Morris stamped her foot. "Yes it is!" she said. "You give back what doesn't belong to you!" Then her voice faded. "Give back, give back," she sang.

She sounded like a child! Freaky! Liz almost handed the key over. "Stay calm,"

she told herself. "I think the key belongs to a woman in Bellport," she said.

"I want it!" said Mrs. Morris. "And you know what else I want?"

Liz took a step back. The moon? Liz's head on a platter?

"I want work! I told your father I'd keep Stone House clean. There's so much clutter in there. It gathers dust!"

She made dust sound like rabies! Liz edged around her. "Ma's waiting," she said.

"I'm going to tell your mother," said Mrs. Morris. "People shouldn't do what they shouldn't do."

There was a crazy look in Mrs. Morris's eyes. She started to sing again, soft and scary. Liz fled down Rocky Point. She felt Mrs. Morris's gaze on her back. Liz kept her eyes on the bed and breakfast—her beautiful white farmhouse, the ocean at the end. Jinx's house came first, a little pointy one painted cream.

Liz heard Mrs. Morris follow her, singing. Maybe Chief was outside! Liz whistled, sort of. She tried to whistle, "Chief, come help me." Hey! Another code that was not Morse code! Liz could use it for Lauren's party list. That is, if she was still alive.

The whistle code worked. Here came Chief. And Jinx. Chief spotted Mrs. Morris. He broke into many barks. "Go away, go away, you stupid woman!" Mrs. Morris stopped. Chief rushed past Liz. Liz looked back. Mrs. Morris turned away. Chief stood in the road. He barked, "I win, I win!"

"She ambushed me!" Liz told Jinx.

"I'll wait awhile before I call Chief

back," said Jinx. "She must really want that key! I wonder why?"

Liz wondered too. "I'm late!" she said. "But do I have stuff to tell you later! Let's all meet at Stone House, okay?"

Ma was up to her elbows in dish suds. "Hi, sweet pea," she said. "Have a nice time?"

Liz could tell Ma wanted to ask about Pop's place. But she also didn't want to hear anything good about it. So Liz just nodded.

"And I saw Mrs. Hall," she said.

"I hope you didn't bother her!" said Ma. "Or ask her about the jewels!"

Now Ma almost sounded like she wanted to pick a fight. Maybe she was just mad because Liz wouldn't talk about Pop's. Liz knew Ma still had hopes Pop would return home. She'd heard Ma tell Aunt Marie so a thousand times.

"Mrs. Hall wants me to find out anything I can about her house," said Liz. "I think she's worried about it. I did ask her about Penny. That made her mad. But she seemed sort of glad too, that I wanted to find her."

"No kidding?" Ma gave Liz a surprised look. "She was glad? What are you, a fairy godmother in training?"

"Maybe," said Liz. She looked at the breakfast dishes. "Too bad I can't do the dishes by magic."

"I'd like it if you'd do the wash by magic," said Ma.

The phone rang. It was Allie.

"Liz? Lauren and Owen McBride are over here. I want them to tell you what they told me."

There were two phones at Allie's house. Soon Lauren got on one, and Owen got on the other.

"Liz?" said Owen.

"It's me. What's up?" asked Liz.

"It's about The Hat Woman," said Owen.

"Allie insisted we call you," said Lauren.

"Lauren and I saw her at that stone house," said Owen.

"She cut some flowers," said Lauren.

"I'm telling it!" said Owen. "And that isn't all. She looked in a tree!"

"Wait," said Liz. "What do you mean, she looked in a tree?"

"In a squirrel hole or something," said Lauren.

"Did she take anything out?" asked Liz. "Like a sack of jewels?" she thought.

"I couldn't tell," said Owen.

"Neither could I," said Lauren.

Too bad. "When were you out there?" asked Liz. Mr. Lee hadn't mentioned seeing any kids this morning.

"Just a few minutes ago," said Lauren. "We were biking around."

"Did you see Mr. Lee?"

"Who's Mr. Lee?" asked Owen.

"Never mind." So The Hat Woman must have returned to Stone House after Mr. Lee left. "Listen," said Liz. "Jinx and Allie and Drew and I are going to Stone House this afternoon. Want to meet out there?"

"I have to watch Owen," said Lauren.

"And Daniel," put in Owen. "You said Daniel could come over too, Lauren!"

"Bring them," said Liz. "Heck, bring the whole island," she thought. They had to find something! They just had to! Before Mrs. Hall died, or Stone House sold, or Mrs. Morris killed her for that key!

Liz washed sheets. She vacuumed. She asked Ma about Mrs. Spencer. Ma didn't remember her.

The Beautiful Marla showed up at noon. She had some news: Her new hair dryer was way cool. Liz watched Ma try not to be angry about the new hair dryer. Ma hated it when Pop bought them new things. She couldn't afford to.

Marla kept talking about Pop. She ate a muffin. Then she washed a spoon. Ma looked more and more tired. Liz went to put more sheets in the washing machine.

Jinx banged on the back door.

"Picnic at Stone House!" he said. "We'll meet the others out there. Here, you take this."

He handed Liz a bag. Liz looked in. Lunch by Jinx could be very good—or very bad. Though it couldn't be worse than the school spaghetti they'd get next week. Jinx's lunch seemed all right so far: sandwiches. Cheese, she guessed.

"Drew's bringing soda," said Jinx. "And

I'll bring some doughnuts."

She should have known. Jinx and doughnuts were like dogs and bones.

"Allie will bring something healthy," said Jinx. "Let's go!"

Liz went. She'd worked two hours. It was Marla's turn.

Liz was hot by the time they reached Stone House. Drew and Allie sat in the shade. Liz put her bike with theirs, in the woods and out of sight. Jinx dropped his on the grass.

Liz handed out sandwiches. When she bit into hers, something crunched. She looked at Jinx.

"Potato chips," said Jinx proudly.

A cheese and potato chip sandwich. Huh. Liz chewed. Not too bad!

"Bring us up to date!" said Allie.

Liz told them about visiting Mrs. Hall and

hearing the phone number at Shady Rest. She told them about her talk with Mrs. Lord on the morning ferry. She told Mr. Lee's story, and how Mr. Lee was looking for a Mrs. Spencer who used to work at Stone House. She told them about The Hat Woman at Stone House and at Beautiful You.

"I thought The Hat Woman was the Stone House gardener," she said. "But she sells shampoo and dried flowers and stuff."

"Maybe she cuts flowers to sell," said Allie.

"Lauren said she cut some flowers this morning," said Liz.

"Wouldn't they die by the time she got them back on the ferry?" asked Drew.

"Cool!" said Jinx. "Dead flowers!"

"Dried flowers," said Allie. "You hang fresh flowers upside down in a dry place, and they dry."

"But why does she come here?" asked Liz. "I mean, why Stone House?"

"Beats me," said Jinx.

A noisy parade biked down Tag-Along Lane. Lauren first, like a mother duck. Then Owen and Daniel. Jinx lit up when he saw Lauren. Liz sent Allie a look.

"Hey! I want food!" said Daniel.

They dropped their bikes near Jinx's. Allie handed over pretzels and grapes. Lauren sat down, and Jinx began to tell her about Penny Hall.

"Where's the tree The Hat Woman looked in, Owen?" asked Liz.

Owen led the way around the side of Stone House. Daniel came too. Liz took a good look at the little rock garden, the narrow lawn, and the trees.

Owen stopped at a pine tree. He pointed to a hole just beyond his reach. Liz reached her hand in. She felt sticks, dry leaves, and nothing else.

"Let's look in all the tree holes!" said Daniel.

"Lauren! We're going to look in all the tree hiding places!" called Owen.

"It's a plan!" said Lauren. "I'll be the tree hiding place general. If you find a tree hiding place, report to me."

"They do the work, and you get the credit," said Jinx. He looked like he wanted to be on the hiding-place crew too.

"Right." Lauren tossed her glossy hair.

"Let's look in the woods," said Daniel. "Penny must have played there all the time when she was little."

He and Owen took off. Lauren sighed and went after them. Jinx watched her. Then he looked like he remembered something.

"Try that key, Liz!" he said. "Didn't Mrs.

Hall want you to find out if it goes to Stone House?"

"Oh, yeah!" Liz tried the key in the front door. It didn't work. They raced for the back door. The key wouldn't even go in.

"No good," said Liz.

"Yoo-hoo!" called the voice she hated to hear. "Is anyone there? Yoo-hoo!"

Mrs. Morris! Liz felt cold with fear. What was it about that woman that scared her so? Those eyes! They were like little black stones under ice!

"Yoo-hoo, children! I heard voices!" said Mrs. Morris.

She was closer! Too close! Liz froze. Drew grabbed her hand.

"Over here!" he hissed.

Drew pulled Liz behind a bush near the cellar doors. Jinx and Allie were already there.

"She's going to find us!" whispered Liz.

"Let her," said Drew. "We have nothing to hide."

A faraway whoop came from the woods. Mrs. Morris stopped. The whoop came again.

"Yoo-hoo!" called Mrs. Morris, this time

to the whoop in the woods.

"Come on!" said Jinx.

He and Drew and Allie headed around the fourth side of the house. But Liz stayed. She had another idea. She pulled out the key. "Please let there be time!" she thought. She put the key in the cellar door lock. It fit! It turned!

She was inside Stone House!

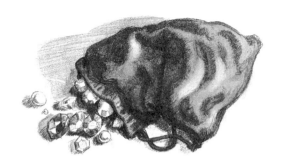

10
HIDE AND SEEK

Liz crept down stairs that led to the cellar.
The cellar was cold and smelled like earth.
Liz saw Jinx's legs through a high window.
She rapped on the glass.

"I'm in!" she hissed. "Go around to the
front where Mrs. Morris won't see you. I'll
open the door!"

Liz made her way up wooden steps.
Spider webs brushed her face. Yuck. She
reached for the doorknob. "Please let it not

be locked!" she thought. The knob turned. Yes! Liz stepped into the front hall. She flew to open the front door. Her friends pushed inside.

"Poor Lauren!" said Jinx. "Mrs. Morris went after her! I hope she can think fast!"

"Owen can," said Drew. "Wow! Would you look at this place!"

"You can tell no little kids live here," said Allie. "Lots of knick knacks, no crumbs!"

Liz ran her hand over the carved knob at

the foot of the stairs. "Gramp said he thought Mrs. Hall hid her jewels in the carvings," she said.

"She could have!" said Drew. "Carved ceilings, carved fireplace!"

"Carved furniture," said Jinx, "like that tall cupboard in the dining room! It has birds and flowers all over it!"

"Let's look for jewels," said Jinx.

"Mrs. Hall wants to know if it looks like anything's been taken from Stone House," said Liz. "And I want to look for clues about where Penny Hall might be. You boys take the downstairs. Allie and I will go up. If anyone sees Mrs. Morris, go bong-bong like a clock."

"Hey, a code that isn't Morse code!" said Jinx.

Liz hurried upstairs to the blue bedroom. It had to be Penny's old room! If she were

Penny Hall, where would she hide important things? In the birdhouse on the dresser? In the bird's nest on the stone window ledge? Behind the horse painting?

Liz moved fast. The birdhouse roof came off. But the birdhouse was empty. Liz took the horse painting off the wall and turned it

over. The back said *From your godmother, Ruth Handy.*

Liz gasped. Mr. Lee once bought a diamond from a woman—a woman Mrs. Hall said might be Ruth Handy! The woman wanted to sell the diamond and give the money to a friend. Was the friend Penny Hall? And wasn't Handy the name of little Penny's pretend friend?

Maybe not so pretend!

Allie came into the bedroom. "Look at this!" she said. She put a green stone into Liz's hand. An emerald?

"Where did you find this?" whispered Liz.

"I picked up this piggy bank," said Allie. She held out a china pig. Fake jewels covered the sides. "That one fell off."

"It's glass!" said Liz. "Isn't it?" She looked again. The green stone flashed like fire. Liz and Allie stared at it.

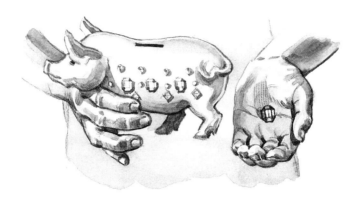

"Maybe Mrs. Hall hid all the jewels like
this," said Allie, "by gluing them in odd
places one at a time! And then she got crazy
and forgot. They could be anywhere! There's
so much clutter!"

"So much CLUTTER," said a voice in Liz's
head. That's what Mrs. Morris had said!
Mrs. Morris wanted to clean Stone House
because clutter gathered dust!

How did Mrs. Morris know about the
clutter in Stone House? Was Mrs. Morris
really Mrs. Spencer?

"Allie! said Liz. "I think Mrs. Morris used to work here! I think her name is really Mrs. Spencer!"

Allie's mouth dropped open. But before she could say anything, loud voices came from outside. Liz beckoned Allie close to a window above the voices.

"Whose bike is that?" said Mrs. Morris's voice.

"That's Jinx Harris's bike!" said Lauren's voice. "You know Jinx!"

"Oh, no!" Liz whispered to Allie. "Our bikes are in the woods, out of sight. But Jinx left his on the grass!"

Drew and Jinx came upstairs. Jinx's face was pale. Liz mimed "Shhh!"

"I'll bet that bad boy is in the house!" said Mrs. Morris's voice outside.

"We were playing hide and seek in the woods!" said Lauren.

119

She wanted Mrs. Morris to think Jinx was in the woods too. The outside voices moved around to the front of the house.

"I'd better get outside," said Jinx.

"You'll give us away!" said Liz.

"No I won't," said Jinx. "I'll go out a far window. You two stay here. Drew, come help me."

Liz thought her heart would fly right out of her mouth. She wished there was still a phone in Stone House. She wanted to call Ma, or Gramp. Or Sheriff Greenwood. She heard a window go up. Now the voices were loud and clear.

"You children are up to something!" said Mrs. Morris's voice.

Now Jinx's voice was outside too. "Hey you guys!" he called. "I win! You didn't find me!"

"Where were you, Jinx Harris?" said Mrs.

Morris's voice.

"Aw, you don't expect me to tell you my hiding place, Mrs. Morris!"

"If you were inside, Jinx Harris, you'll be sorry!" said Mrs. Morris.

Her voice got smaller. Drew must be easing the window down. Liz and Allie crept down the stairs to join him.

"They're leaving," whispered Drew. "Jinx, Lauren, the kids—"

"Mrs. Morris?" asked Liz.

"She's watching them leave," said Drew.

"You mean she's still out there?" Liz asked.

"She's still out there," said Drew.

11

THE MYSTERY OF STONE HOUSE

Liz told Drew her idea that Mrs. Morris was Mrs. Spencer.

"Maybe she wants the key you found so she can get inside!" said Drew.

"Maybe she's the one who took the jewels!" said Allie.

"I want to call Pop," said Liz. "And Mrs. Hall. But we can't leave as long as Mrs. Morris is out there!"

The knob rattled on the front door. Mrs.

Morris! Liz's mouth felt dry. She, Allie, and Drew ducked down. One sound and they were done for! Mrs. Morris pressed up to the window beside the door.

"I could break a window!" Liz heard her say, "and blame it on those kids!"

Mrs. Morris left the door.

"She's getting a rock," guessed Drew.

Liz started to shake. In a minute Mrs. Morris would be inside too!

"Guys!" she said. "What if Mrs. Morris comes in after the jewels?"

"Wait," said Drew. "If she stole the jewels, wouldn't she have them?"

"Oh, yeah," said Liz. "And Mr. Lee said that Mrs. Spencer got fired before the jewels were missing."

"So maybe Mrs. Morris—who is really Mrs. Spencer—just wants to look for the jewels," said Allie.

"Wait!" said Liz. "What if she hid the jewels—and planned to steal them later?"

"Explain," said Drew.

"What it she replaced the real jewels with fakes so no one would guess," said Liz. "Because she planned to steal the real jewels. But she got fired!"

"Before she had a chance to get the jewels out of the house!" said Allie.

Drew caught on. "And then Mrs. Hall found the fake jewels!" he said.

"Right! And Mrs. Hall thought Penny took the real ones!" said Allie.

"Because Penny had just run away!" finished Liz.

"That's it!" said Drew.

They all looked at each other.

And then they heard the sound of breaking glass.

Liz swallowed a scream. "She'll find us!"

she said. "Let's leave!"

A thump came from the back of the house. More glass broke. Liz's heart beat double-time with fear and excitement.

"Wait," said Allie. "It sounds like she's trying to get in the cellar," she said. "Let's hide and watch. If we're right, she'll go straight to the jewels, because she knows where they are!"

Drew slid into the hall closet. Allie squeezed behind a sofa. Liz ran for the carved cupboard in the dining room. Maybe she could fit inside. She heard a bang from the cellar, and muttered words. Mrs. Morris was in!

Liz reached the cupboard. The door stuck. "Please, please open!" She heard Mrs. Morris start up the cellar stairs.

The cupboard door opened. Tablecloths inside! Liz pushed them sideways.

Stomping and muttering, Mrs. Morris came upstairs.

Liz pushed her way into the cupboard. She pulled the door almost shut.

Just in time. The cellar door opened. Liz saw Mrs. Morris step into the hall.

"All my pretties," said Mrs. Morris.

She sounded crazy! Liz was scared to watch. She was scared not to. She saw the woman run her hand over each stair rail. She twisted each one. Then the carved knob at the bottom of the stairs came right off. Mrs. Morris peered inside.

"Empty, empty," she crooned.

Was that where Mrs. Hall used to keep her black velvet bag? Liz held her breath.

"Give back," sang Mrs. Morris.

She went out of sight. She came back after about a minute, humming. She had something in her hand.

127

"One-two, sapphire blue!" she sang.

Liz watched her pick up a china vase.

"Around back!" cried a voice from outside.

Jinx!

"Who is that?" Mrs. Morris's voice was sharp with fury. She went to a window. "That boy! They'll have to climb in. Just like me!"

Liz gasped. Mrs. Morris wheeled at the sound. She stared right at the cupboard. Right into Liz's eyes. Liz almost fainted. Mrs. Morris stamped her foot.

"No!" she said. "No! No! No!"

She picked something up from a bowl on the table. Liz thought it looked like a brass egg. A heavy brass egg. Mrs. Morris raised the thing over her head. She came for Liz. Liz had nowhere to go.

"Help!" she screamed.

Help came. Allie came from behind the sofa. Drew came from the closet. Jinx came from the cellar. Someone else was behind Jinx.

It was Mrs. Hall's nurse!

"Mrs. Spencer!" said the nurse.

Mrs. Morris stopped. Liz didn't know why the nurse was there, but the nurse knew who Mrs. Morris was! Liz's guess was right—

Mrs. Morris was really Mrs. Spencer!

Mrs. Morris tried to look everywhere at once. She turned around and around. She still had her arm up, ready to hit someone with her brass egg. Drew grabbed her arm from behind. Mrs. Morris started to cry.

"All my pretties!" she said. "I've waited so many years for them!"

The nurse looked at Mrs. Morris with eyes full of pity. "Hello, Mrs. Spencer," she said.

Mrs. Spencer looked at the nurse. Her mouth opened. She dropped three stones from her hand.

"Jewels!" said Jinx. He picked them up.

Liz crawled out of the cupboard. The nurse came and helped Drew hold Mrs. Spencer.

"No, no, no!" said Mrs. Spencer "Not me, not me! Penny Hall!"

"You know Penny Hall didn't take the jewels," said the nurse gently.

"Then where is she?" said Mrs. Spencer. Her voice was shrill and mean. "If Penny Hall is so good, how could she leave her sick old mother?"

"She couldn't," said the nurse.

Liz turned to the nurse. Did she know Penny Hall? Liz looked at the nurse's kind eyes. Those eyes could love anyone: Mrs. Hall, Mrs. Spencer. Little hurt birds.

"You're Penny Hall!" Liz said.

12

Proof of Magic

The kind nurse nodded. "Yes, Liz," she said. "I'm Penny Hall."

Someone pounded on the front door. Jinx ran to open it. In came Sheriff Greenwood. He looked big and square and safe. Liz was glad to see him.

Sheriff Greenwood nodded to the nurse. "Hello, Penny," he said. "Welcome home. I'll take charge of the suspect. Meet me at my office when you're done here."

He took Mrs. Spencer's arm. Mrs. Spencer slumped.

"All my pretties," she said sadly.

Now she sounded like a child. Liz felt sorry for her. She watched Sheriff Greenwood take Mrs. Spencer out the front door.

Then she watched Mr. Lee walk in.

He was with The Hat Woman.

"What's going on?" asked Drew.

Liz looked from Mr. Lee to The Hat Woman to Penny Hall. "Do you all know each other?" she asked.

"We didn't know Mr. Lee until today," said Penny Hall. "Tanya came here this morning to look for a key she had lost. It was a key I'd given her, on a key chain my father gave to me."

"Are you Tanya?" Allie asked The Hat Woman.

"Yes," said The Hat Woman.

"I have your key," said Liz. "I tried to return it to you at Beautiful You. I showed it to Mrs. Hall too. She told me to see if it fit Stone House and to check on the house for her."

Liz gave Tanya the key.

"But who are you?" asked Jinx.

"I'm Penny Hall's foster daughter!" said Tanya. "Years ago, my own mother and I were homeless. Penny Hall took us in. After my mother died, she raised me! Aunt Penny is the best, the kindest, the most wonderful woman alive! And that Mrs. Spencer is the most cruel!"

Penny Hall put her hands on The Hat Woman's shoulders.

"It's all right, Tanya," she said. "It's all over now."

Tanya said, "Aunt Penny's mother blames her for something she didn't even do! But Aunt Penny is so good that she dyed her hair gray. She put on fake glasses and changed her name. All to care for her mother at Shady Rest!"

Penny Hall took over the story. "Mother got a little careless about the jewels in the year before Dad died," she said. "Dad was so sick, you see! He wanted mother to put the jewels in a bank. She wouldn't. When I heard the jewels were missing, I thought maybe Dad hid them, and then died before he told Mother where!"

Tanya added, "I tried and tried to find them after Mrs. Hall went to the nursing home. I searched the house high and low, but never found a pile of jewels. I didn't think of looking for single jewels! So I began to search the grounds."

"That's where I come in," said Mr. Lee. "This morning I watched Tanya look into trees and bushes around the house. She ran away from me, twice! I did not want to scare her. So I caught up with her at the ferry landing, where there were lots of people and she could feel safe."

"Mr. Lee and I talked," said Tanya. "And then I called Aunt Penny."

"Penny rode the ferry over," said Mr. Lee. "Then we met Jinx and Sheriff Greenwood on the way to Stone House. Jinx had quite a story to tell!"

"And I figured out the mysterious Mrs. Morris was really Mrs. Spencer," said Penny Hall.

"And—the jewels?" asked Mr. Lee.

Jinx handed him the stones Mrs. Spencer had dropped. Mr. Lee took a lens from his pocket and peered at them.

"Genuine," he said. "Sapphire. Sapphire. Ruby."

"Emerald?" asked Liz.

She handed Mr. Lee the stone Allie had

found. Mr. Lee nodded.

"The jewels must all be here!" said Allie. "She stuck them in places like this!"

She pointed to the china vase that Mrs. Spencer had picked up. China flowers covered it. Liz saw that each china flower had a glass center.

Or were they diamonds?

"We'll help you look for your jewels!" said Jinx. "We're good at solving puzzles!"

Mr. Lee looked at Penny Hall. "Would you like that?" he asked. "I have the list."

"Yes, please," she said. "Oh, it's so good to be home!"

"Where did you go?" Jinx asked her.

"Years ago, when you left Ragged Island?"

"I'll bet I know!" said Liz. "You went to visit Ruth Handy!"

Penny nodded. "Ruth Handy was my godmother," she said. "She was so good to me! She's dead now, but back then she took me right in. And she sold some of her things to pay my way through nursing school!"

"Like the diamond from her ring," said Mr. Lee. "Now we know who the woman was who brought the diamond to my store," he said to Liz.

There was one more thing Liz wanted to know.

"Does Mrs. Hall—your mother—know who you are?" she asked Penny Hall.

Penny Hall smiled. "No," she said. "I've gained weight, you see. And I wear padding at work to look bigger. I dyed my hair, and

I wear glasses. But she likes me, you know. She's much nicer to me than to anyone else at Shady Rest. And after you came, Liz, she cried. I said, 'Mrs. Hall, you miss your daughter, don't you?' And she nodded. So I know that deep inside, my mother still loves me."

Penny Hall smiled a beautiful smile brighter than any jewel. Liz's eyes filled with glad tears. Because here was the thing she had been looking for all along—proof of magic!

SCAVENGER HUNT LIST

1. A frog, but not a real frog.

2. A jewel, but not jewelry.

3. A code, but not Morse code.

4. A book, but not a reading book.

5. Music, but not recorded music.

6. Something alive that's smaller than a quarter.

7. A wheel, but not a toy's wheel.

8. Proof of magic.

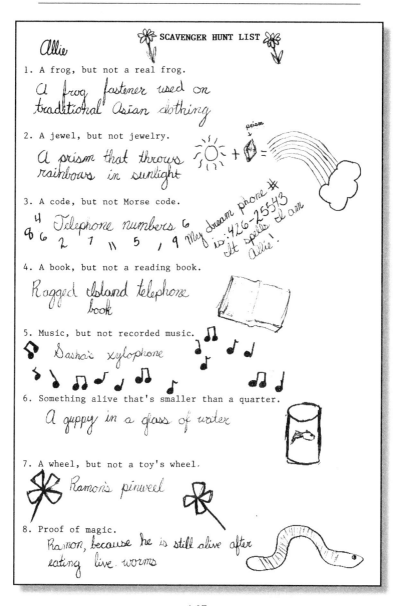

🌼 SCAVENGER HUNT LIST 🌼

Allie

1. A frog, but not a real frog.

A frog fastener used on traditional Asian clothing

2. A jewel, but not jewelry.

A prism that throws rainbows in sunlight

3. A code, but not Morse code.

Telephone numbers

My dream phone # is: 426-25543. It spells it out. Allie.

4. A book, but not a reading book.

Ragged Island telephone book

5. Music, but not recorded music.

Dasha's xylophone

6. Something alive that's smaller than a quarter.

A guppy in a glass of water

7. A wheel, but not a toy's wheel.

Ramon's pinwheel

8. Proof of magic.

Ramon, because he is still alive after eating live worms

143

SCAVENGER HUNT LIST

Jinx

1. A frog, but not a real frog.

   Tape recording of fake frog "ribbet"

2. A jewel, but not jewelry.

   A piece of sea glass

3. A code, but not Morse code.

   Tape recording of the ferry blasts

4. A book, but not a reading book.

   A checkbook

5. Music, but not recorded music.

   A harmonica

6. Something alive that's smaller than a quarter.

   A spider

7. A wheel, but not a toy's wheel.

   Steering wheel from a junked car

8. Proof of magic.

   The one spelling test I ever aced

SCAVENGER HUNT LIST

Drew

1. A frog, but not a real frog.

A recording of a frog in my throat

2. A jewel, but not jewelry.

A photo of Ragged Island — a "jewel" in Mackerel Bay

3. A code, but not Morse code.

A list of catcher's signals for the pitcher from my league team.

4. A book, but not a reading book.

A photo album

5. Music, but not recorded music.

A coffee can filled with beach pebbles and water (when I turn it upside-down it sounds like rain)

6. Something alive that's smaller than a quarter.

A live snail in a jar of seawater

7. A wheel, but not a toy's wheel.

A photo of a Ferris wheel

8. Proof of magic.

A tomato that I grew from seed

145

SCAVENGER HUNT LIST

Liz

1. A frog, but not a real frog.

A frog-shaped pencil sharpener

2. A jewel, but not jewelry.

A deep blue perfume bottle, borrowed from The Beautiful Marla

3. A code, but not Morse code.

Chief's barking code

4. A book, but not a reading book.

A notebook

5. Music, but not recorded music.

Whistling "Chopsticks"

6. Something alive that's smaller than a quarter.

A tiny flower in a tiny pot

7. A wheel, but not a toy's wheel.

Tanya's hat, borrowed

8. Proof of magic.

Penny Hall (and) Mrs. Hall forgave each other

About the Author

Michelle Dionetti loves mysteries, old wooden boxes, singing, subways, drawing, ancient Egypt, painting, and traveling anywhere she's never been before. She is athletic—that is, in her mind. She lives on the coast of Maine with her husband, who also writes. They have too many books—if there were such a thing as too many books. Her recent books include *Mice to The Rescue* and *Painting the Wind*.